BOMB!

BOMB!

JIM ELDRIDGE

With illustrations by
Dylan Gibson

Barrington Stoke

To Lynne, my inspiration as always

First published in 2011 in Great Britain by
Barrington Stoke Ltd
18 Walker Street, Edinburgh, EH3 7LP

www.barringtonstoke.co.uk

This edition first published in 2013

Text © 2011 Jim Eldridge
Illustrations © Dylan Gibson

ISBN: 978-1-78112-305-8

Printed in China by Leo

Contents

Chapter 1
The Bomb

TOP SECRET REPORT

Time: 9:15 a.m.

Subject: Bomb alert

A terrorist rang MI5 yesterday and said

that he was going to explode a bomb at

a school today. The bomber asked for a ransom of £5 million, or he would set the bomb off at 10 a.m.

He also said that he will explode the bomb by remote control if it is found and anyone tries to defuse it.

The bomb has been found hidden in the boiler room of Adam High School. It is not known if the bomber is aware that the bomb has been tracked down.

All schools in that area are now closed. Pupils were told that there was a study day for teachers.

The other schools are all bringing cleaners in as normal, so as not to make the bomber suspicious.

A bomb disposal expert, Rob Dean, will go into Adam High School dressed as a cleaner. He is only 19, but he is the best the army has. He has 45 minutes to make the bomb safe.

Chapter 2
A Dirty Bomb!

Rob Dean got out of the van and looked at the school building. He wore a blue overall with "Ace Cleaners" on it. The same words were written on the side of the van. But Rob was not a cleaner – he was a bomb disposal expert. Beneath the blue overall he was wearing body armour.

It was now quarter past nine. Rob had 45 minutes to stop the bomb going off.

Rob walked slowly up to the main door of the school as if he was in no hurry to get to work, just in case the bomber was watching the school.

But as soon as he was inside the building he began to run. He rushed down the stairs to the basement. Every minute that passed was a step nearer the bomb blowing up!

Rob got to the boiler room. The bomb was where MI5 had said it would be. He looked at the digital display on the bomb. It was counting down the minutes. It showed 44 minutes to go before it went off.

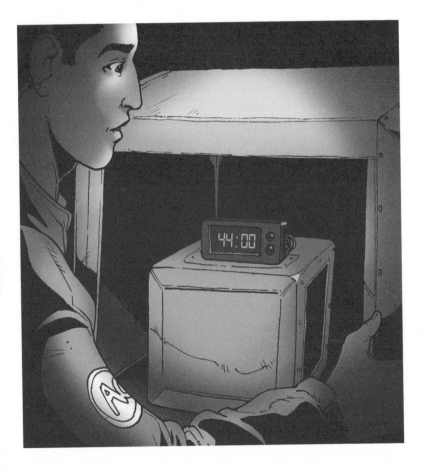

Rob took his helmet from inside his vacuum cleaner, which was where he had hidden his tools, and put it on. He pulled out his goggles and a face mask, in case there was gas inside the bomb.

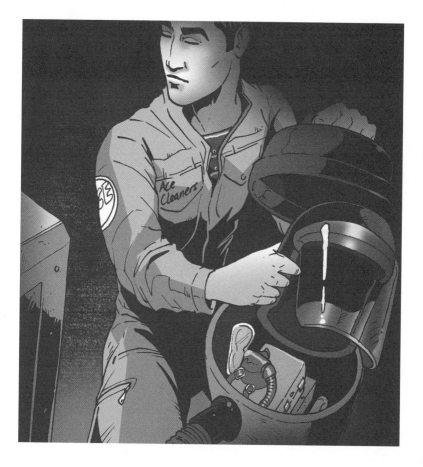

There was a microphone inside the face mask, attached to a tiny digital recorder, so he could log in details about the bomb. This was important. If Rob was killed when the bomb blew up, then someone would listen to the recording and work out what he had done just before it exploded. The recorder was made of some strong stuff which could withstand bomb blasts.

"Report from Rob Dean," he said and gave the date, time and place.

Rob had been with the Bomb Squad for six months. In those six months he'd defused three bombs. Two had been old bombs from World War Two that had been found buried in a wood. One had been a terrorist bomb filled with nails that had been left in a bag on a bus.

His best friend at the Bomb Squad had been Tom Watts. Tom was 21 and had been working on bomb disposal for three years.

Last month Tom had gone out to deal with a bomb left by some terrorists at a railway station. The bomb had gone off as Tom had been working on it. Tom had been killed at once.

Many things could go wrong when you tried to defuse a bomb. Some bombs had booby-traps inside them. If you touched the wrong wire, or pressed the wrong button, they blew up.

'That bomb must have been booby-trapped,' thought Rob. Tom had known everything there was to know about bombs. Or maybe the terrorists had come up with a new kind of detonator.

"Is this bomb booby-trapped?" Rob asked himself.

He examined the bomb with care. It was a square-shaped metal box with a display on top. The number on the display was counting down to zero. The wires and detonators must be inside the box. The box had been fixed firmly inside a larger metal container. There was a gap at the top. Rob shone a torch into the container. He could see lots of test tubes in it. They were filled with a yellow liquid.

Suddenly Rob saw what the plan was. When the bomb exploded it would smash the test tubes and whatever was inside them would be blown out.

There could be anything in those test tubes. Germs. Killer bacteria. Radiation. It didn't help that this was a basement. The force of the explosion would smash the windows. The stuff inside the test tubes would escape into the outside air and would

kill thousands of people. He was dealing with

a dirty bomb!

Chapter 3
The Trigger

If Rob had had more time he would have

taken the metal box from the container and

moved the test tubes somewhere safe. But

he didn't have time – he only had 35 minutes.

The metal box was fixed firmly into the

container. The only way to get it off would

be with cutting tools. That would take him

a long time. And if the bomb was booby-trapped, any movement might set off the detonator.

"We are dealing with a dirty bomb," he said into the recorder. "It looks like test tubes of germs packed under the detonator. The detonator is inside a small metal box with a digital display on it. The display shows there are 34 minutes before it goes off."

'The first thing to do is to open up the device,' thought Rob. 'Get a look at the trigger mechanism.'

Rob began to undo the screws that held the plate around the digital display in place. As he turned the screwdriver, he felt sick deep inside.

If the bomb was booby-trapped, this would be one of the first places a trap would be set. Sometimes electrical wires were joined up to screws inside the metal plate, so that if a screw was taken out the electrical connection was broken, and the detonator would go off.

Rob took out the first screw gently. It came out cleanly. 'So far so good,' he thought. Three more screws to go. He knew that any one of them could be the booby-trap.

The second screw came out. Then the third. Very gently, he undid the last screw. He took it out. Nothing happened.

Rob breathed a big sigh of relief.

He felt the metal plate with great care. It was now loose. Slowly he began to lift one side of the plate about one or two millimetres. He looked into the gap. There didn't seem to be any wires holding the plate to the bomb, but it was dark inside the box.

Rob shone his torch into the gap between the plate and the detonator. He was always tense at this stage and had to grit his teeth to stop his hands shaking. Sometimes trigger sensors inside bombs were set off by light, and they would explode when a torch was shone on them.

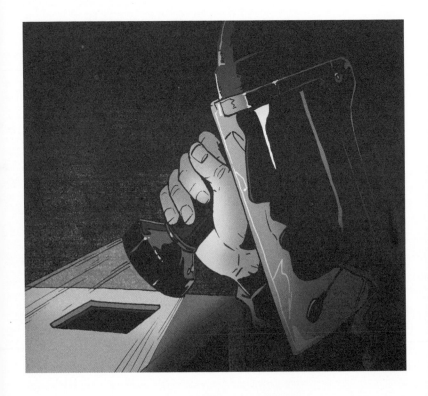

Nothing happened. This one seemed OK so far.

With great care Rob lifted the plate off and exposed the trigger device.

Inside it was a mess of wires and timer dials. Two thin copper wires went from the timer to a small battery.

'The bomber said he would blow the bomb up if anyone tried to interfere with it,' Rob thought. 'That means it must have a second detonator that can be triggered from a distance by a mobile phone.'

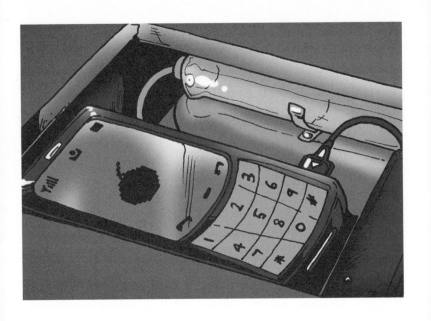

Yes, there it was. There was an old mobile phone wired to the trigger.

Rob took a small piece of electronic gear from the vacuum cleaner. It was a mobile phone jammer, which would stop phone calls from going in or out anywhere near the bomb. He placed it next to the mobile phone by the detonator. That would stop the

detonator being set off by a phone call. The problem was, it also meant that Rob couldn't use his own phone.

Rob checked the display. It was still counting down. There were only 21 minutes left. It had taken him a long time just to get the cover plate off.

Chapter 4
Booby-Traps

Rob looked at the small battery. He could disconnect it, and then the count-down clock would stop. But sometimes these clocks were set so that if they stopped suddenly they went to zero. If the count-down clock went to zero that would trigger the bomb and it would explode.

It would be safer to leave the count-down clock working at this moment. He would see if he could stop the count-down clock from setting off the explosives.

Rob examined the wires which connected the timer to the explosive charge. There were six wires. They were different colours. One was blue, one was brown, one was green, one was yellow, one was black, one was red. 'I must cut the wires. But which ones? All of them?' he thought.

Suddenly a thought flashed into Rob's mind. What had happened to Tom when he was killed? He had been working on a bomb, and the detonator had been connected to the explosive charge with six wires.

Those wires had been different colours: one blue, one brown, one green, one yellow, one black, and one red. This was the same sort of trigger device!

Rob tried to remember what Tom had said on the tape he had recorded when he'd been trying to defuse the bomb.

He could remember listening to Tom's voice saying, "I am cutting the blue wire."

There had been the sound of the clippers cutting the wire. Then Tom had said, "I am cutting the green wire." And again there had been the sound of the clippers cutting the wire. But what was the colour of the wire that Tom cut next? Because it had been the next colour wire that had set the bomb off.

Rob tried to remember. It was hard. Because he'd been so upset about Tom being killed he'd shut all the details out of his memory. Tom had said which colour wire he was cutting next. There had been the sound of the wire cutters, and the next sound had been a huge explosion.

Listening to that tape had been awful for Rob. Hearing his best friend die. But that was why Tom had recorded what he was doing, in case that happened. So that other people could be saved.

Rob checked the timer. There were 13 minutes left.

How could he find out which of the wires was the killer one?

One way would be to phone his Head Office and ask them to play the tape of Tom's last message. Ask them which colour wire Tom had cut through just before the bomb blew up.

But to do that Rob would have to switch off the mobile phone jammer. And if he did that, the bomber could set the bomb off by remote control, using the mobile phone inside the bomb.

Also, it would take time for Head Office to find Tom's last message and play it.

If this bomb was exactly the same as the one Tom had tried to make safe, then the blue and green wires were OK.

That left the brown, the yellow, the black and the red. One of those was the wire Tom had cut that had set the bomb off. Which one was it?

Chapter 5
Which Wire to Cut?

Rob spoke into his recorder. "This looks like the same sort of detonator that killed Tom Watts. The wires have six different colours. They are blue, green, brown, yellow, red and black. If it is the same, then the order could be the same that Tom tried. I shall follow what he did. I am about to cut the blue wire."

Rob used his wire cutters to cut the blue wire.

Nothing happened. The count-down timer carried on counting down. It now showed 11 minutes. Nothing exploded.

If this was the same sort of bomb that had killed Tom, Rob expected the blue and green wires to be safe. But sometimes things changed. The bomber could have changed the order of the wiring.

Rob gritted his teeth.

"Let's hope this really is the same sort of detonator Tom worked on," he said to himself.

"I'm about to cut the green wire," he said into the recorder.

Rob cut the green wire. Again, there was no explosion. The count-down now showed 10 minutes to go.

"There are four wires left. Brown, yellow, black and red," said Rob. "I can't remember which one Tom cut next, but that was the one that killed him. There are 10 minutes left to go before this bomb explodes. I cannot use my mobile to phone Head Office for advice, because I have put a phone jammer by the detonator, to stop the bomber setting it off by remote control. I will have to guess which order to cut the wires."

Rob examined the four wires that were left. They went from the explosives to the timer clock. If he undid the panel at the back

of the timer clock he might be able to see

where the ends of the different wires went.

He guessed that two of the wires were the triggers for the explosives. Either of the other two wires could be the booby-traps, put there to short circuit the timer clock and trigger the explosives if they were cut.

Brown, yellow, black or red?

Rob took a small screwdriver and began to unscrew the tiny panel at the back of the timer clock itself. All the time he was tense in case these screws were booby-trapped, but they came out without anything going wrong.

He used the screwdriver to prise off the small panel.

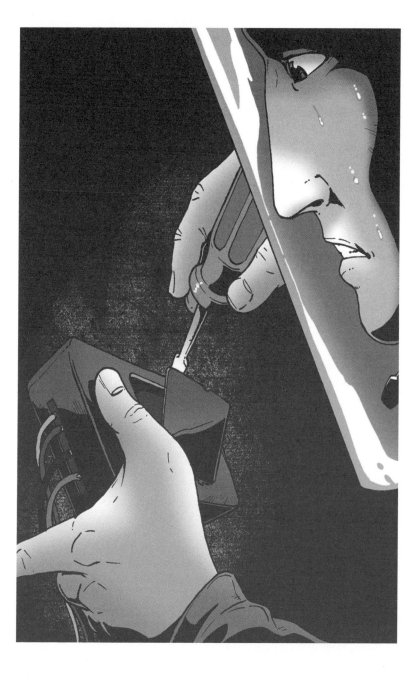

There were three wires connected to the workings of the timer. Brown, red and yellow. Where was the black wire? It went into the bottom of the timer with the other three, but it wasn't connected to the workings of the clock itself.

Rob peered into the tiny space, looking for the black wire.

There it was! It was attached to the metal inside the digital display.

The good thing was, the black wire didn't connect the timing clock to the explosives, so he didn't have to worry about it. It wasn't part of the booby-trap. That left the brown,

the red and the yellow wires. Two of them
were safe to cut. The other one was the
booby-trap. Rob guessed that if it was cut or
removed it would set the clock to zero. And
then the bomb would blow.

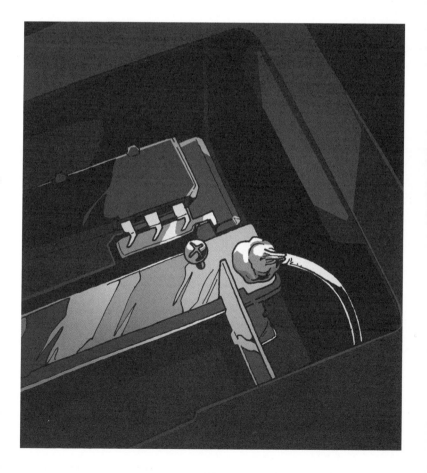

Into his microphone Rob said, "The black wire is soldered to the side of the metal casing of the clock. The booby-trap wire is either the brown, the red or the yellow."

Rob looked at the count-down clock. It showed 3 minutes left.

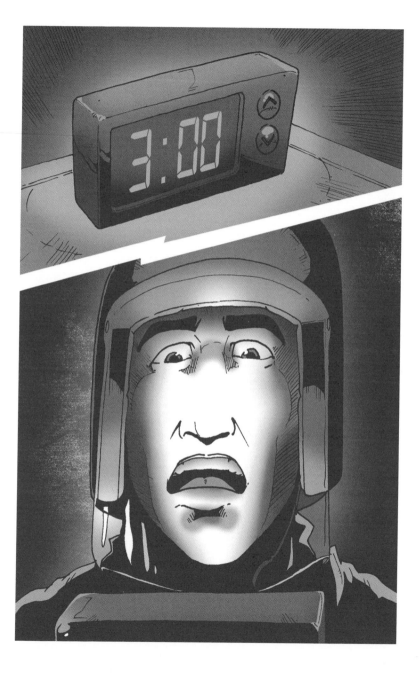

Chapter 6
60 Seconds Left!

Rob studied the three wires. At the same time he tried to remember Tom's voice on the recording. Which colour wire had Tom cut?

He closed his eyes and took himself back to one month ago. He was sitting in the office with his boss and the other members of the Bomb Disposal Unit. They were listening to Tom's voice.

"I am cutting the blue wire." The sound of the clippers cutting. Then Tom saying, "I am cutting the green wire." The sound of clippers again. Then Tom saying, "I am cutting the ..."

Rob tried hard to remember. Which colour had Tom said? Brown, red or yellow?

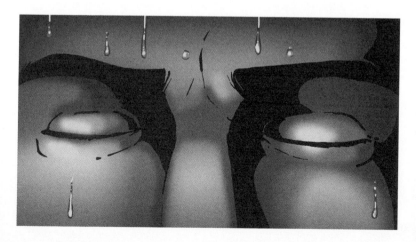

Yellow! He was sure it was yellow!

The explosives needed two wires to make the connection. So cutting the brown or red wires should cut the connection between the clock and the explosives.

"I think the yellow wire is the booby-trap," Rob said into the microphone. "I am cutting the red wire."

Rob couldn't stop his hand from trembling as he put the sharp edges of the wire cutters on either side of the red wire.

Snip!

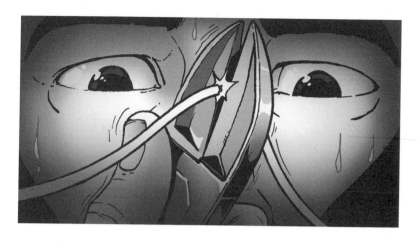

The count-down clock continued. Two minutes to go.

"Just to make sure, I am also cutting the brown wire," said Rob.

He put the blades of the wire cutters on either side of the brown wire, and cut.

Only the yellow wire now linked the timer to the explosives.

The digital display showed one minute.
Then 59 seconds. 58. 57. 56 ...

"Only the yellow and black wires haven't
been cut," said Rob into his microphone. "If I
was wrong, then whoever deals with this sort
of bomb next needs to know that. We'll find
out in a very short while. The count-down is
now reading 9 ... 8 ... 7 ... 6 ... 5 ... 4 ... 3 ... 2 ...
1 ...

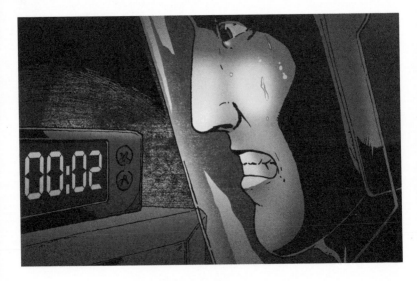

The display went to zero.

Nothing happened.

Rob let out a very long sigh of relief.

"The bomb has been disarmed," he said.

Our books are tested
for children and young people by
children and young people.

Thanks to everyone who consulted on
a manuscript for their time and effort in
helping us to make our books better
for our readers.

Also by **Jim Eldridge**...

Under Attack

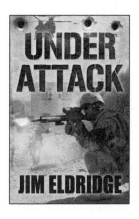

INCOMING! TAKE COVER!

Dr Sari Patel and Captain Joe MacBride are under fire!

The Taliban attack the hospital
Sari and Joe are building.

A young girl is hurt by a bomb.

Joe must draw fire away from the village while
Sari performs the most dangerous operation of
her life.

Can Sari and Joe hang on in there?

www.barringtonstoke.co.uk

More from *Barrington Stoke*...

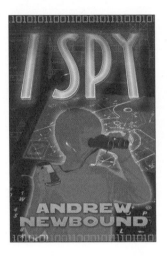

I Spy
ANDREW NEWBOUND

Finn borrows his spy dad's top secret work gear to become 'School Spy'.

When Tom gets bullied, he calls on Finn to help him out.

Can Finn and Tom beat the bullies together?

Hostage (4u2read)
MALORIE BLACKMAN

"I'll make sure your dad never sees you again!"

Blindfolded. Alone. Angela has no idea where she is or what will happen next. The only thing she knows is she's been kidnapped. Is she brave enough to escape?

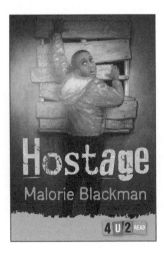

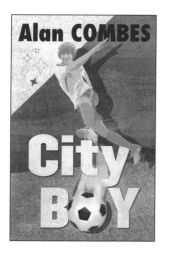

City Boy
ALAN COMBES

Josh loves football – but he needs to get much better to play for City.

His grandad has a plan.

Can he help Josh get to play for his heroes?

United Here I Come!
ALAN COMBES

Jack and Jimmy are very bad at football.

But Jimmy is sure he will play for United one day.

Is Jimmy crazy – or can he make it?

www.barringtonstoke.co.uk

This Igloo book belongs to:

. . . .

. . . .

Reading Together

This story is written in a special way so that a child and an adult can 'take turns' in reading the text.

The left hand side is for the adult to read.

The right hand side has a simple sentence (taken from the story) which the child reads.

Once upon a time there was a merchant who had three daughters.
The youngest daughter was called Beauty. They all lived in the country.
One day the merchant had to go into the town.
Beauty asked her father to bring her a pink rose.

Beauty asked her father to bring her a pink rose

Firstly, it is always helpful to read the whole book to your child, stopping to talk about the pictures. Explain that you are going to read it again but this time the child can join in.

Read the left hand page and when you come to the sentence which is repeated on the other page run your finger under this. Your child then tries to read the same sentence opposite.

Searching for the child's sentence in the adult version is a useful activity. Your child will have a real sense of achievement when all the sentences on the right hand page can be read. Giving lots of praise is very important.

Enjoy the story together.

I Can Read...

Beauty and the Beast

Once upon a time there was a merchant who had three daughters.
The youngest daughter was called Beauty. They all lived in the country.
One day the merchant had to go into the town.
Beauty asked her father to bring her a pink rose.

Beauty asked her father to bring
her a pink rose.

The merchant went to town.
On the way back it started to rain.
The merchant got lost in the woods.
The merchant found a huge old castle.
He went inside.

The merchant got lost in the woods.

There was no one in the castle. But there was dinner on the table and a warm fire. The merchant ate the food and went to sleep.

When he woke up he remembered that he had promised to take Beauty a rose.

There was no one in the castle.

The merchant went into the garden
of the castle. He picked a pink rose.
The merchant heard a loud roar.
He saw a huge, ugly beast.
"That is my rose!" said the Beast.

The merchant heard a loud roar.

The merchant said he was sorry.
He explained that the rose was a present
for Beauty.
"I will spare your life if Beauty will
come and live with me," said the Beast.

The merchant said he was sorry.

When the merchant got home he told
Beauty what had happened.
Beauty said she would go and live
in the castle.
When Beauty met the Beast she
was surprised.
He was kind to her. Beauty and the
Beast soon became friends.

Beauty and the Beast soon
became friends.

Beauty missed her father and sisters.
The Beast said she could go home.
Beauty promised she would only stay at
home for a week.
But Beauty liked being at home so
much she forgot her promise.
Beauty did not go back to the castle.

Beauty did not go back to the castle.

One night Beauty had a dream.
Beauty dreamed that the Beast was
very ill.
She hurried back to the castle.
The Beast was dying of a broken heart
because he missed Beauty so much.

Beauty dreamed that the Beast
was very ill.

Beauty realised she loved the Beast.
She started to cry. Her tears fell on the
Beast's face. WHOOSH!
The Beast was changed into a
handsome Prince.

The Beast was changed into
a handsome Prince.

The Prince explained that a wicked fairy
had put a spell on him. The spell turned the
Prince into the Beast.
Beauty's tears had broken the spell.
Beauty and the Prince fell in love.
They lived happily ever after in the castle.

Beauty and the Prince fell in love.

Key Words

Can you read these words and find them in the book?

rose

Beauty

merchant

Beast

castle

Questions and Answers

Now that you've read the story can you answer these questions?

a. Who asked her father to bring her a pink rose?

b. Whose meal did the merchant eat in the castle?

c. Where did Beauty go to live with the Beast?

a. Beauty   b. The Beast's meal   c. The castle

Tell your own Story

Can you make up a different story
with the pictures and words below?

house

merchant

woods

sisters

Beast

horse

fell in love

castle

Mix and Match

Draw a line from the pictures to the
correct word to match them up.

rose

Beast

castle

Beauty

merchant

horse

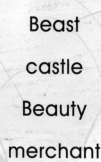